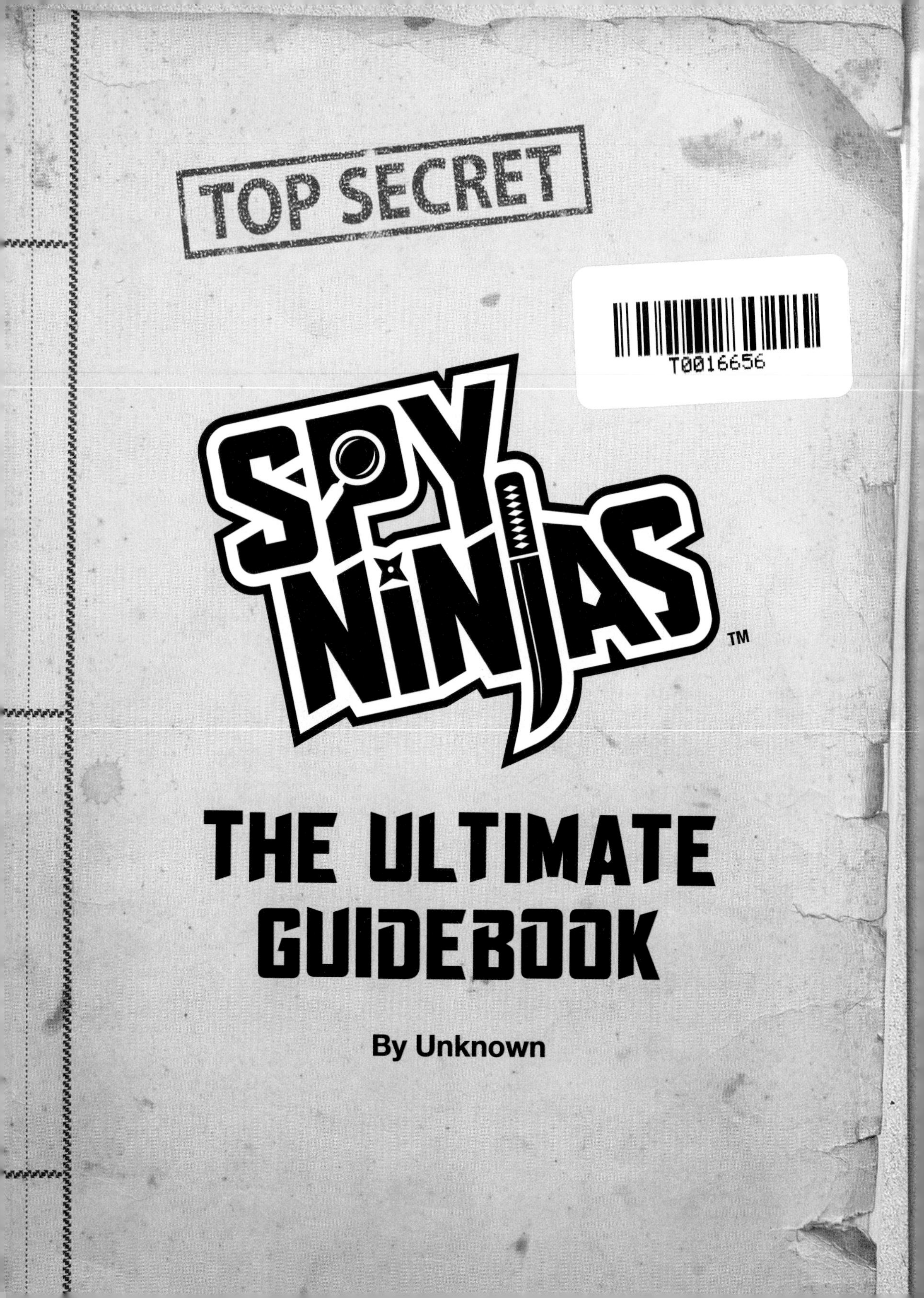

THE ULTIMATE GUIDEBOOK

By Unknown

Photos © Shutterstock.com and Textures.com.

ISBN 978-1-338-80578-9

10 9 8 7 6 5 4 22 23 24 25 26

Printed in the U.S.A. 40

First printing 2022

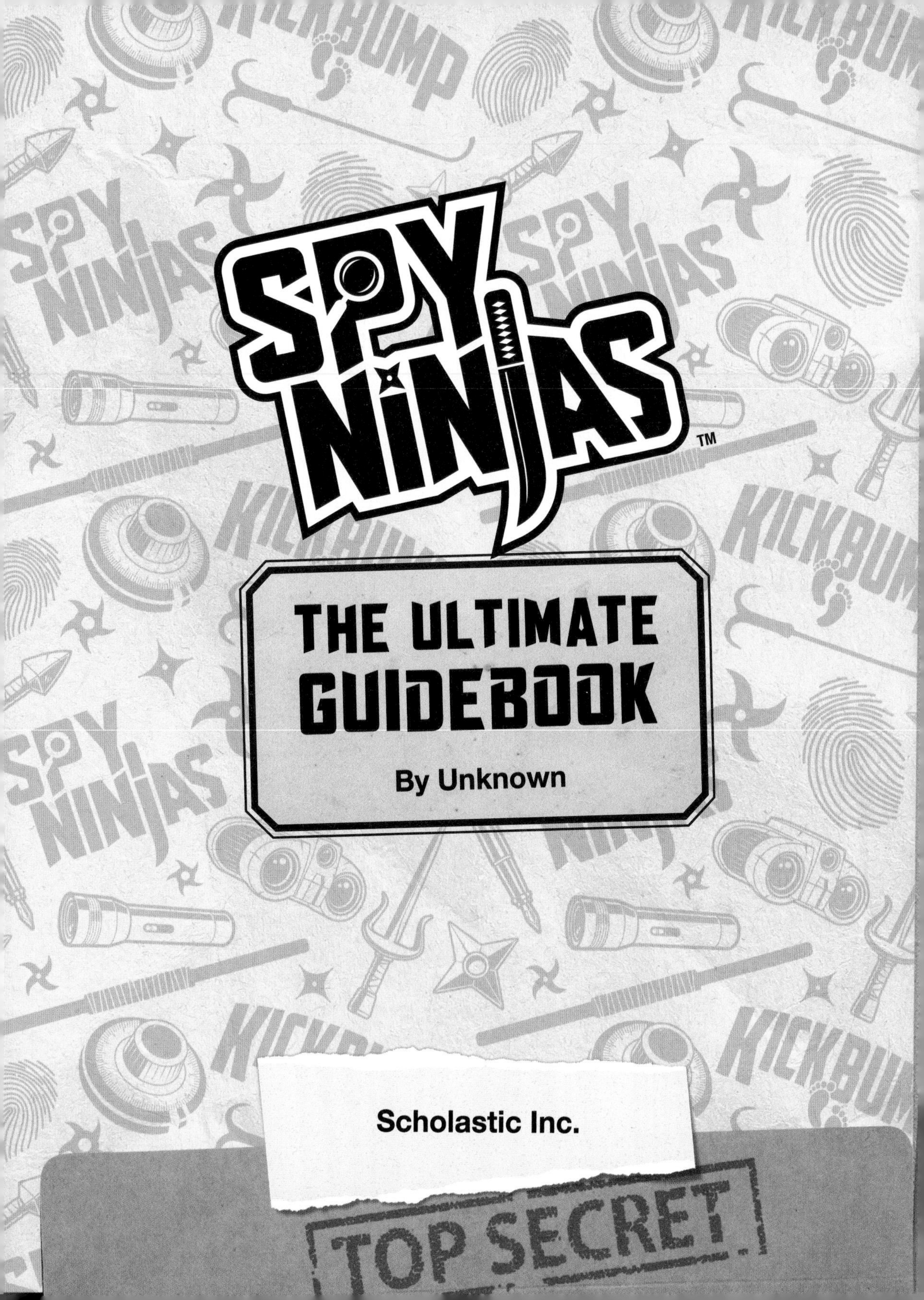
SPY NINJAS™
THE ULTIMATE GUIDEBOOK
By Unknown
Scholastic Inc.
TOP SECRET

SPY NINJAS™
PROJECT ZORGO

If you're reading this book, you're probably a little like me: You've watched the Spy Ninja's awesome videos, maybe you even want to BE a Spy Ninja, and you're hoping to learn more. In this guide, I'm going to download EVERY ESSENTIAL PIECE OF HISTORY you need to know about Chad, Vy, and their team of Spy Ninjas. So, what are you supposed to do with that information?

Well, that depends:

Are you an aspiring **SPY NINJA?**

A hacker, from **PROJECT ZORGO?**

Or are you just a curious onlooker who's really into SOLVING MYSTERIES, SCAVENGER HUNTS, EPIC NINJA BATTLES, and mind-blowing YOUTUBE VIDEOS?

And who am I? Well, that's not information I'm prepared to share. (A good spy never spills their secrets.) But I WILL share everything you need to know about the essential Spy Ninjas history, and you can use this information however you see fit. Just use it the BEST way . . . or else.

TOP SECRET

So, who ARE the SPY NINJAS?

They are a team of brave, curious, and funny YouTubers on a mission to stop PROJECT ZORGO, an evil organization of hackers who are trying to take over YouTube and the internet.

The Spy Ninjas—led by founding members CHAD WILD CLAY and VY QWAINT—combine martial arts, puzzle-solving and spy skills, sneakiness, and computer hacking to uncover and stop Project Zorgo's secret mission. They film their adventures, battles, and challenges in order to share them with fellow Spy Ninjas and YouTube followers—so their millions of fans can help investigate, solve problems, and decode mysteries alongside Chad, Vy, and the team.

Have you been following along with the Spy Ninjas from the very beginning, or are you new to their channels? Did you start watching because you want to help . . . or want to hack?

I know more about the Spy Ninjas than anyone—maybe even more than Chad and Vy themselves. After all, I've been watching and studying them for years. Who am I? Let's just say that's . . . confidential.

But here's what I can tell you: After you finish reading this book, you will have one important thing to decide . . .

Are you WITH the Spy Ninjas or are you AGAINST them?

The choice is yours. Just make it the RIGHT one.

TOP SECRET

WHO ARE THE SPY NINJAS?

CHAD

SPY NINJAS

CHAD WILD CLAY

Chad developed his skills with ninja gadgets by chopping fruit and sodas.

FAVORITE FOOD: Tacos

FAVORITE GADGET: Transforming Stun-Chucks

FAVORITE NINJA MOVE: Tornado Kick

VY

SPY NINJAS

VY QWAINT

As the tiniest Spy Ninja, Vy can go undetected where others can't and is great at hiding in the smallest of spaces.

FAVORITE FOOD: Hot Cheetos

FAVORITE GADGET: Secret Message Spy Pen

FAVORITE NINJA MOVE: Double Roundhouse Kick

DANIEL

SPY NINJAS

SN

DANIEL GIZMO

Daniel is a self-proclaimed expert on many things and is the team's technology expert.

FAVORITE FOOD: Footlong Subs

FAVORITE GADGET: Gizmo Drone

FAVORITE NINJA MOVE: Spinning Arm Throw

SPY NINJAS

REGINA

SPY NINJAS

SN

REGINA GINERA

Clumsy and dramatic, Regina is a former hacker and a master of disguise.

FAVORITE FOOD: Chicken Nuggets

FAVORITE GADGET: PZ Voice Morpher

FAVORITE NINJA MOVE: Flying Jump Kick

SPY NINJAS

MELVIN

SPY NINJAS

SN

MELVIN PZ9

A former Project Zorgo hacker, Melvin's values of fame and friendship led him to join the Spy Ninjas.

FAVORITE FOOD: Spinach

FAVORITE GADGET: Covert Communicator

FAVORITE NINJA MOVE: Butterfly Kick

SPY NINJAS

TOP SECRET

NINJA GADGETS!

TRANSFORMING STUN-CHUCKS
Transforms from a baton to nunchucks!
Stun your opponents!
SECRET MESSAGE SPY PEN
Invisible Ink! Secret Message Compartment! UV Light for Revealing Hidden Messages!
SPY NINJAS

PZ VOICE MORPHER
PROJECT ZORGO
Disguises your voice to impersonate Project Zorgo!
COVERT COMMUNICATOR
SPY NINJAS
Walkie-talkie, ninja star launcher, compass, mirror & magnifying glass, all on your wrist!
KICKBUMP
SPY NINJAS
TOP SECRET

CHAD WILD CLAY

Chad became well-known on YouTube for unboxing ninja gadgets seen in video games and movies, and testing them out like a "Fruit Ninja" in real life. He's an expert with ninja gadgets. Hi-yah! Ninja and martial arts skills come in handy when Project Zorgo hackers challenge Chad to a battle royale!

Chad has tested a TON of cool gadgets and weapons over the years, including:

Silver Finger Claws vs. Emoji Water Balloon
Bow Staff vs. Mr. Pepper

Hand Flame Throwers vs. Emoji Balloon

Every once in a while—but not very often—Chad shows his weaknesses. Like the time this happened while he was testing nunchucks:

Vy is the tiniest Spy Ninja, and her size comes in handy for sneaking into the smallest of spaces when she and the team are tracking hackers and solving puzzles. Vy loves using her spy skills to pick locks, build handy gadgets out of household items, and solve clues that help stop the evil hacker group Project Zorgo. Vy was best known for her fashion, beauty, and lifestyle videos on YouTube but switched over to focus on Spy Ninja missions after she and Chad discovered a hidden crawl space in their Los Angeles apartment!

Bladed Fan
vs.
Bananas

DANIEL

Daniel is the Spy Ninja team's TECH WIZARD, who often uses his gadget watch, flying drone, and hacking skills to keep an eye on Project Zorgo's activity so the Spy Ninjas can stop their hacking missions. He is also the team's LIE DETECTOR EXPERT and can almost always determine if someone is telling the truth or a lie. That skill really comes in handy!

REGINA

Regina is an expert computer hacker and a master of disguise. She loves using the Spy Ninjas' Project Zorgo voice morpher and a hacker mask to fake being one of the bad guys to get important intel. Regina is sometimes a little clumsy and overly dramatic, which can cause some problems for her.

Melvin is a former hacker and expert fighter. Ultimately, his biggest dream in life is being famous . . . with a side of friendship. These two things are what made him decide to join the GOOD guys instead of sticking with Project Zorgo. Melvin longs to someday be the world's most popular YouTuber and doesn't like following other people's rules.

TOP SECRET

KEY PROJECT ZORGO MEMBERS

PZ FUNF: The leader of Project Zorgo's gaming division. No one knows if this is true, but he CLAIMS he's from Germany . . . and loves bratwurst. He often uses his fingers to make horns on his head so he can bull-charge one of the Spy Ninjas while hollering out his catchphrase: ***HEE HEE!***

PZ2: Project Zorgo's hacking division leader. No one knows why PZ2 is so small and hunched over . . . or why he makes sounds like a dog. He can sneak through the tiniest spaces, just like Vy, and despite his small size, he can jump high, and he claps when he's excited.

PZ SQUIRE: This member of Project Zorgo's gaming division is not old enough to go out on real-life hacker missions, so his job is to hack video games to help Project Zorgo get control of the internet. Though he ACTS tough, PZ Squire is nothing but talk, talk, and more talk.

PZ LEADER: No one knows much about PZ Leader . . . just that this guy is all evil, all the time.

TOP SECRET

THE ORIGIN OF SPY NINJAS: ESSENTIAL HISTORY

A few years ago, Chad and Vy's normal YouTube videos had to be put on hold after Vy found a HIDDEN CRAWL SPACE behind a speaker inside the wall of their apartment in Los Angeles, California. Because they love solving mysteries, Chad and Vy decided they absolutely MUST explore the tunnel to see if it led anywhere cool. Since she's the tiniest human Chad knows, Vy gets nominated to be the one who got to crawl inside the tiny space.

"It's really useful being a tiny ninja!"
—Vy Qwaint

I Found an Abandoned SAFE and Hidden Secret Tunnel

Inside the tunnel, Vy finds a KEY that unlocks a door Chad and Vy haven't been able to get open ever since they first moved into their apartment.

At first, it seems like the door was just hiding a boring old storage closet—but then Chad and Vy spot a LOCKED SAFE hidden inside a box.

After trying to crack the safe for hours, Chad feels a little foolish when he finally figures out the mystery code to open it:

$100,000 ABANDONED SAFE
Mystery Box Unboxing Challenge
Congratulations!
Inside this safe you will find clues that will lead you to $100,000 of hidden treasures. Hopefully figuring this out won't Drive you crazy!
But they ALSO find another, smaller safe that holds a note . . .
a bunch of clues . . .
A TOY CAR?
THERE ARE NO WHEELS!
WHAT IS THIS?!
MODEL X
. . . and a map that promises to lead them on a SCAVENGER HUNT to find a $100,000 PRIZE!
The map leads them to Palm Springs!
YOUR TREASURE AWAITS IN
Palm Springs
ADMIT ONE

FOUND $100,000 ABANDONED TESLA

When they get to Palm Springs, the Spy Ninjas find an abandoned TESLA MODEL X. At first, they wonder if maybe *this* is their prize . . . but that seems WILD! Who just gives someone a car?

The duo finally get into the Tesla, and that's when they discover their next big surprise: They're TRAPPED! Has this whole scavenger hunt been a TRICK to trap Vy and Chad so someone can hack their YouTube channels?! All signs point to YES.

TRAPPED in $100,000 ABANDONED TESLA for 24 HOURS CHALLENGE

I HOPE IT'S YOUR CHANNEL AND NOT MINE.

This video has been removed

The pair of Spy Ninjas frantically pull up Chad's YouTube channel, and that's when they realize one of their favorite YouTube videos is GONE.

And to make matters even WORSE, they're TRAPPED inside the Tesla and have to spend 24 hours inside the car.

Being trapped inside a car by some unknown and unseen enemy is weird, but what happens next is even weirder. In the morning, the Tesla starts driving itself to an abandoned zoo!

While the Tesla drives them to their next destination, Chad and Vy receive a message on the car's video screen:

Depending on which secret underground tunnel they choose, the hacker will make them complete one of these challenges:

Crack an egg over their heads

Delete another favorite YouTube video

Eat a tarantula spider

SPY NINJA CHALLENGE:

If YOU were one of the Spy Ninjas, which of these challenges would YOU choose?

LET'S FIND THIS HACKER!

After a second video is deleted from Chad's channel, he and Vy decide it's time to go searching for the hacker—they're sick and tired of this happening and they need to put an end to it.

Using maps stored in the Tesla's memory, they manage to find the . . .

EXPLORING SECRET VAULT & TRAPPED in HIDDEN UNDERGROUND ABANDONED HACKER TUNNEL with PUZZLES!

Inside the hacker's house, Chad and Vy find mysterious vaults.

The Spy Ninjas nervously poke around inside both these vaults and discover that one of them leads to a door locked with a padlock. They decide there MUST be something good hidden behind something so well protected!

But before they can get through the locked door, they need to figure out: WHAT DO ALL THESE SYMBOLS on the back of all these mousetraps MEAN?

The Spy Ninjas solve a series of clues and use a decoder wheel to figure out what code they need to unlock the door. The code is ZORGO.

Behind the locked door, they find the hacker's laptop computer and a map of the hacker's location!

WHAT WOULD YOU DO IF YOU WERE A SPY NINJA?

Would you: **Follow the map to find the hacker?**

Leave everything as you found it and hope you don't get caught snooping?

The Spy Ninjas decide it's time for a huge adventure, so they follow the map to a dusty field filled with CLUES, like:

These dirty gloves (gloves that look very familiar):

Some cool spy goggles:

A rubber chicken key chain that lays eggs when they squeeze it:

A cell phone, with a lock screen of the letter *J*:

WHO'S J?!

TOP SECRET

A cool voice changer:

A whole bunch of weird metal letters and coins:

While they're digging up clues, the Spy Ninjas realize they might be in some danger. Luckily, Chad brought along his backpack filled with some of their favorite ninja gadgets, like a pair of nunchucks for Chad and Vy's metal staff!

TRANSFORMING NINJA STAFF!

Ultimate weapon in super-spy gear! A secret compartment for messages, and strobe lights to distract hackers!

What the Spy Ninjas don't seem to realize is, through all their adventures, someone has been tracking them—the same way they are tracking the hacker.

Luckily, Chad and Vy are smart enough to know they better watch their backs!

After thinking about all the clues they've found on this quest, the Spy Ninjas begin to suspect that the hacker was HERE before them—the gloves and voice changer are definitely Project Zorgo, all the way! But the hacker must have left empty-handed because it's Chad and Vy who manage to find the treasure the hacker was probably here looking for: a buried treasure chest!

TOP SECRET

FOUND ABANDONED TREASURE CHEST HIDDEN UNDERGROUND w/ SECRET MAP

After Chad tries—unsuccessfully—to bash it open using his ninja nunchucks, the Spy Ninjas head home to try to open the chest and find out what's inside. Their next set of clues leads them to an old, abandoned town.

To keep both himself and Vy safe, Chad grabs his SPY NINJA BACKPACK full of gadgets and weapons, just in case they run into any trouble.

But instead of finding the hacker or anything else dangerous, Chad and Vy discover even more strange clues that bring them closer to figuring out who this mysterious hacker is.

WHAT THEY KNOW SO FAR:

The hacker's name starts with a J.

He owns a CWC hat.

The newest clue: He has a BEARD!

Keep in mind, while Chad and Vy are conducting their investigation, someone is tracking their every move! A true Spy Ninja always has to be aware of their surroundings.

While exploring the abandoned town, Chad and Vy run into some SERIOUS trouble.

DID YOU KNOW?

Chad and Vy's longtime friend, who used to film Fruit Ninja videos with them, has a beard and his name starts with J.

WHO COULD BE KEEPING SUCH A CLOSE EYE ON THE SPY NINJAS?

After Chad and Vy finally escape the town, they find an old-fashioned cassette tape with a secret message recorded on it. But it's not until they find a SECOND cassette tape, and realize they need to listen to the two messages TOGETHER, that they get their next clue!

HACKER TRACKER!

By decoding the messages on the cassette tapes, Chad and Vy head to an address to see if they can finally figure out the identity of this mysterious hacker. When they find a hacker mask on a training dummy inside the house, it's clear they're finally on the right track. This must be where the hacker lives!

Using Ninja smarts to figure out clues that are hidden in a collection of playing cards, they manage to open a locked door.

FOUND HACKER after CRACKING into SECRET ABANDONED NINJA Dojo to Reveal a Secret

After months of searching, have Chad and Vy finally . . .

NINJA WEAPONS

Which would YOU choose if you were going to confront the hacker?

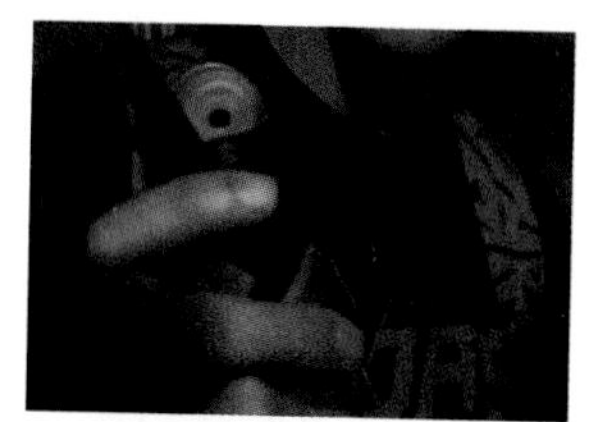

Flashlight Weapon

Chad's Trusty Sais

The Spy Ninjas decide it's time to confront this guy face-to-face. But when they get close, they realize the hacker is tied up.

So Chad pulls off the hacker's mask and is shocked to discover the hacker is his childhood friend Justin!

Chad is totally thrown off—he thought he and Justin were best friends! How could his best friend turn on him like this? They used to make videos together, and they even took karate and ninja classes together when they were kids!

CWC vs. HACKER in Real Life NINJA BATTLE ROYALE

As soon as Chad unties him, Justin attacks. The two duke it out in the ultimate **NINJA BATTLE ROYALE**.

That's when Justin accuses Chad of KIDNAPPING him! Eventually, the Spy Ninjas and Justin all realize they've been duped. Justin was tricked by the hacker and framed to make it look like HE was the hacker all along. Good thing Chad and Vy found him and freed him, or he might have been stuck, tied up at the hacker's house forever! Yikes!

Justin tells his friends he overheard the hacker saying he only trusts his dog to keep his keys. And that the keys open a safe where he's hidden SECRET DOCUMENTS!

RIPPING OPEN ABANDONED SAFE vs. SPY GADGETS and EXPLORING HAUNTED FOREST at SHARER FAM HOUSE

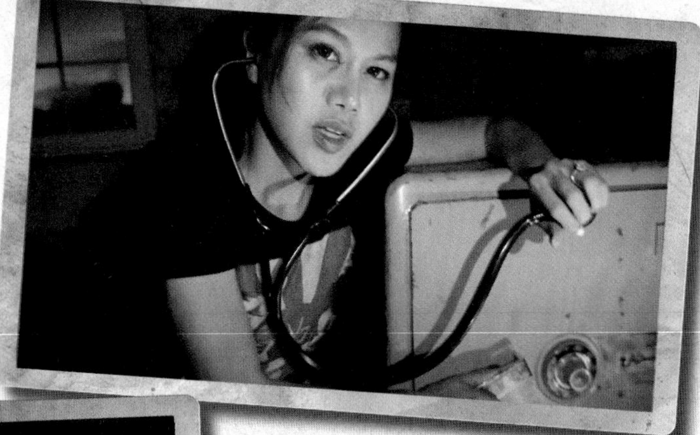

They decide to enlist the help of some other YouTubers to try to uncover who the REAL hacker is. But first, they end up helping to crack open a safe at the Sharer house using Vy's super-Ninja safecracking skills!

She can't figure out the combo using her stethoscope and safecracking hacks, so Vy ends up trying to see if she can figure it out by using the INVISIBLE LIGHT in her Ninja backpack.

After they see this symbol, Chad and Vy are hunted by someone—or something—and Chad gets sucked into a water drainage system. He wakes up in an abandoned hospital, where he's trapped in a room all alone—with no answers about where he is or how he got there.

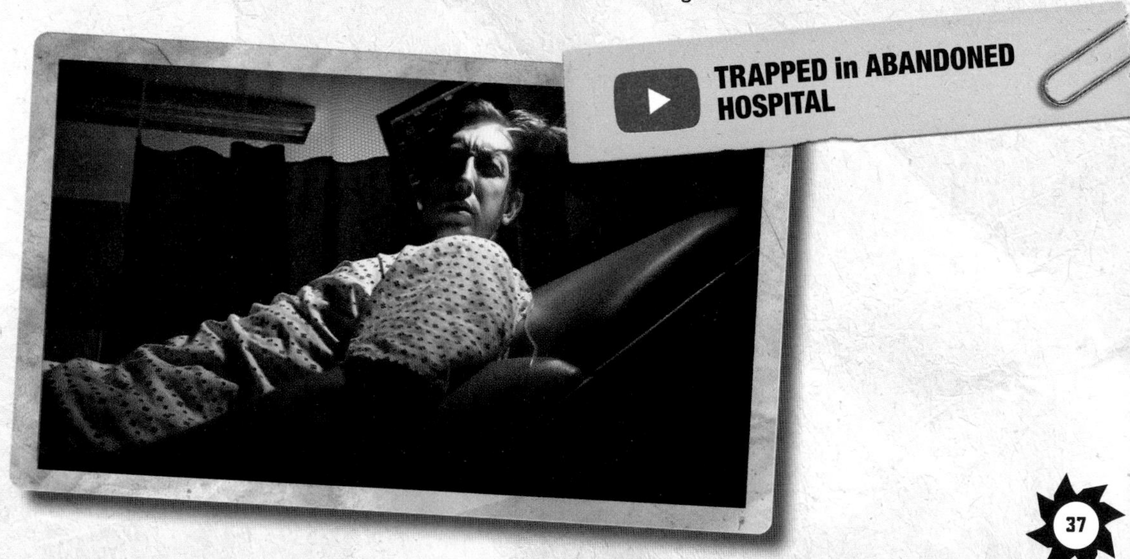

TRAPPED in ABANDONED HOSPITAL

WHO IS THE HACKER??

While they're trying to figure out the identity of the hacker, Chad decides he might as well have some fun, so he plays a prank on Vy using their copy of the hacker mask.

IS CHAD WILD CLAY The HACKER in Real Life?

Even though Vy is super annoyed, Chad gets a big kick out of his joke. But it's not so funny a few minutes later when their pizza is delivered by someone else wearing a hacker mask! Does the real hacker KNOW WHERE CHAD AND VY LIVE?? After all their pranks on each other, Chad and Vy start to get suspicious of each other—what if one of them actually is the hacker? Then they find some suspicious cameras and tracking devices hidden under the floorboards! They start fingerprinting items in their house to see if someone other than one of them has been inside their home.

SPY NINJA TIP:

If you want to lift fingerprints off a suspicious item, you:

1) Gently lay a piece of clear tape (sticky-side down) over the whole fingerprint.
2) Press firmly, to make sure the print transfers to the tape.
3) Voilà! Now you've lifted the fingerprint off the item and can save the print on a piece of paper where it won't get smudged while you investigate further.

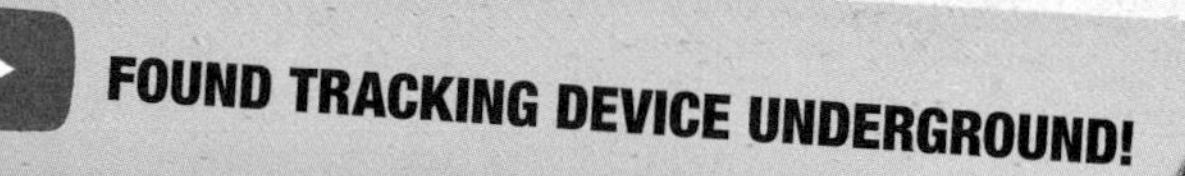

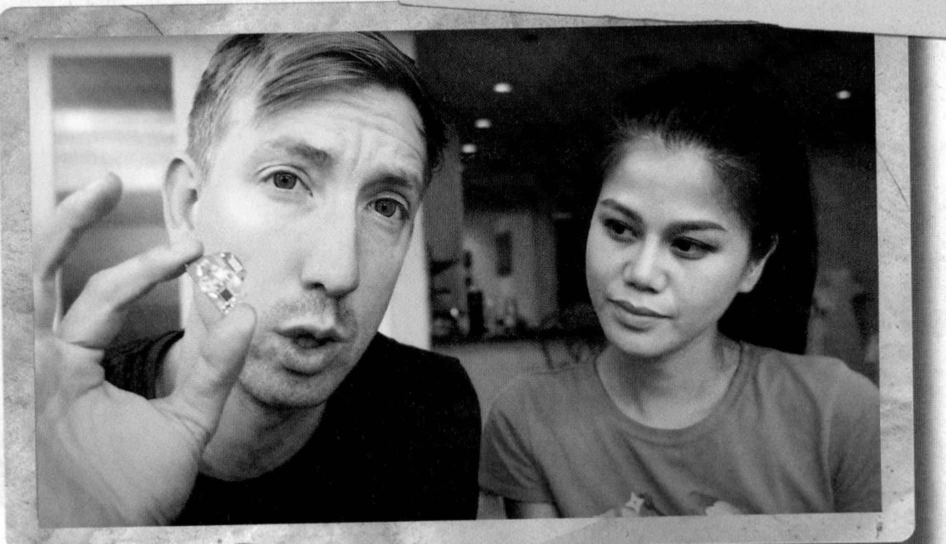

That's the lie detector guy!

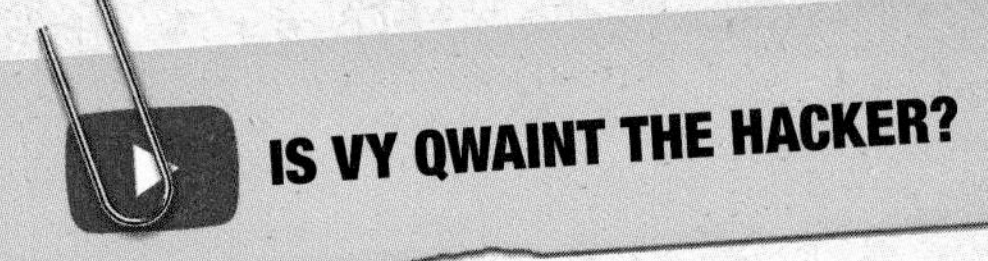

IS VY QWAINT THE HACKER?

Ultimately, Daniel the Lie Detector Guy determines it's definitely not Chad or Vy who is the hacker. But if it's not one of them pranking the other, who IS the hacker? Why can't they solve this mystery?

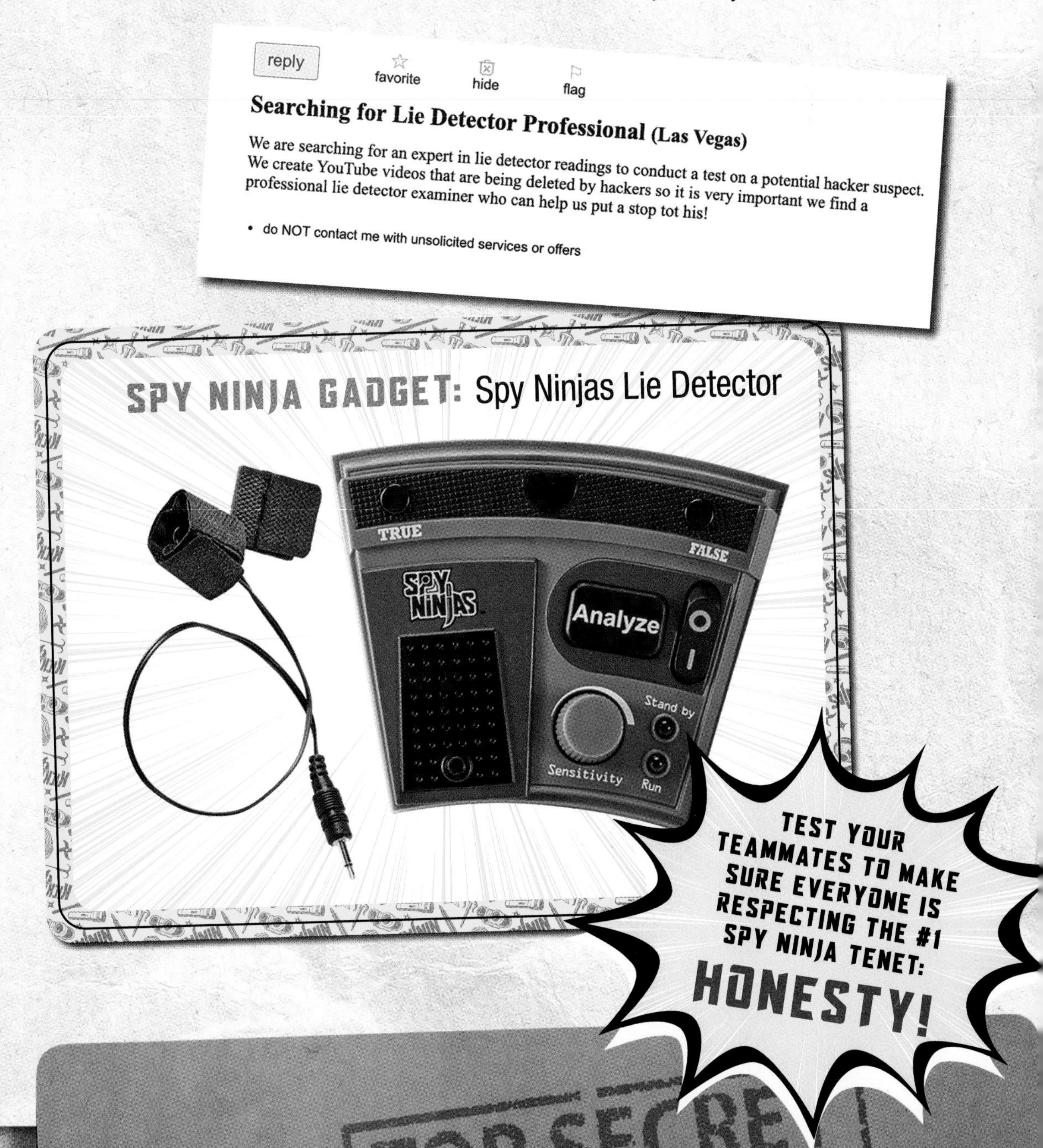

reply favorite hide flag

Searching for Lie Detector Professional (Las Vegas)

We are searching for an expert in lie detector readings to conduct a test on a potential hacker suspect. We create YouTube videos that are being deleted by hackers so it is very important we find a professional lie detector examiner who can help us put a stop tot his!

- do NOT contact me with unsolicited services or offers

INTRODUCING: PROJECT ZORGO

JOIN OUR TEAM OF YOUTUBE HACKERS!
YOUTUBE MUST BE STOPPED
Downloading...
Critical Data

Chad and Vy manage to get their hands on the hacker's phone and discover—by investigating through the contacts—that there's not just one hacker . . . there are more than a dozen! And all of them use the code name **PZ**. Chad decides to pose as a hacker and get in touch with some of these PZ hackers so he and Vy can do a little hacking of their own. They come up with a plan to **REVERSE HACK** the other hackers' computers so they can track them back to their hidden lair!

But at the same time, the Spy Ninjas start to stumble upon strange notes around their house.

These papers just so happen to have been found underneath items that the LIE DETECTOR EXPERT was suspiciously touching. Hmmm . . .

Chad and Vy decide to follow the lie detector guy to see if they can figure out what is going on.

Using a **SPY NINJA LISTENING DEVICE:** Chad and Vy overhear the lie detector guy mention the name ZORGO. All evidence is starting to suggest that Daniel the Lie Detector Guy is DEFINITELY the hacker!

TO PZ 1,

I can't believe you're thinking of quitting Project Zorgo. You can't! We're just getting started. How am I supposed to continue here without my most trusted colleague! Now I gotta deal with PZ 2 by myself?! PLEASE RECONSIDER! Chad & Vy have to be stopped & YouTube needs to be taken down. I saw you pretend to be a lie detector guy and go to their home. You better not have done anything stupid or revealed our plans! PZ1 PLASE DON'T QUIT!

- Ur most trusted colleague,

PZ 4

While they're on this latest spy mission, Chad and Vy discover another treasure chest! Chad manages to break this one open with his Kusarigamas, and inside it they find another note. This handwritten note matches up with some of the others they've found, but they still don't know what it all means. Slowly, more elements of the mystery are coming into focus, but they have a long way to go before they can uncover and stop this hacker, once and for all!

10:32

HACKER TAKEOVER!

The day Chad and Vy have been dreading finally arrives! The hackers are trying to take over the Spy Ninjas' HOUSE by entering through the **HIDDEN CRAWL SPACE**!

PROJECT ZORGO HACKED Our HOUSE in Real Life

Chad and Vy scare the intruder away for a few minutes, leaving them just enough time to put all their ripped notes together to reveal a message.

To Chad and Vy,
I work for the hacker and it is very important that you know I am on your side and trying to help you.
Your entire house is bugged and we can see and hear everything you do. I'm doing this for your own good.
When you are ready, say the following code word and never come back

Using a special spy light, they uncover an invisible message at the bottom of the note that says they need to shout the code word *MR. SKYLIGHT* . . . and leave the house, with no plans to ever come back.

As soon as Chad and Vy shout the code word, the house lights and electronics start going totally nuts, and a countdown timer plays on the speakers. Horrified, Chad and Vy rush out of their house—and immediately realize they'll probably NEVER have the opportunity to return home again.

NOWHERE TO GO

Hoping to get away from all the hacker activity and the dangers lurking inside their very own house, Chad and Vy decide to drive to Las Vegas. On the way there, they open and read the letter Vy stole out of the lie detector expert's backpack while they were tracking him.

The letter reveals that the lie detector guy is trying to QUIT Project Zorgo because he thinks that Chad and Vy are actually good people and that they—and other YouTubers—don't deserve to be hacked. The letter is addressed to someone named **PZ4.**

While they're searching for clues in an abandoned old ghost town, the Spy Ninjas find part of a broken hacker mask, then use their spy skills to track some mysterious-looking footprints.

FOUND PROJECT ZORGO FOOTPRINTS & HIDDEN NOTE

While they're hunting for more clues, they also discover a letter and other hints that suggest someone named PZ1 is in trouble . . . who is PZ1, and where are they now?!

It was a success but now,
Project Zorgo is after me!
I don't have much time left
before I go off the grid.
I just hope they can find my clue
in the [illegible]. It will help them.
Bridge

Chad and Vy find a map that leads them to a mysterious abandoned house.

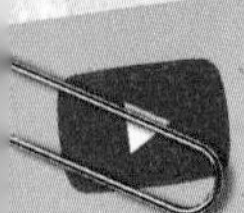

TREASURE MAP Led Us to an ABANDONED SAFE HOUSE

When they get inside the house, there is a message waiting for them:

For now you're safe
Until it turns 8pm
Turn off the lights
Stay out of sight
Don't even yawn
Until it's dawn

The Spy Ninjas have a feeling the hackers will show up at the house sometime after 8:00, so they decide to set some traps, hoping to catch them in the act! Through their spy cams, they spot a dark figure sneaking around the house—trying to get in! Is it the hackers?!

DID YOU KNOW?

The Spy Ninjas are used to having to stay up late because a popular YouTube trend is to stay up until 3 a.m. to see if something spooky happens.

CAUGHT HACKER BREAKING INTO ABANDONED SAFE HOUSE on Camera

CAM 1 DOOR

But here's the strange thing: Whoever this mysterious figure is has delivered a little surprise for Chad and Vy. It's a box full of ninja weapons and spy gadgets! Is this suspicious character a FRIEND or an ENEMY?

Do YOU remember?

SPY NINJA GADGETS:

Night-Vision Mission Kit

NIGHT-VISION GOGGLES!
REMOVABLE FLASHLIGHT!
GADGET UTILITY BELT!
DECODER WHEEL!
SPY NINJA RED LENS READER!

TOP SECRET

All of Chad's old Fruit Ninja practice definitely comes in handy after they open their MYSTERY BOX of ninja gadgets, along with the following message:

MYSTERY BOX

"Use these weapons like a Fruit Ninja to find out secret information!"

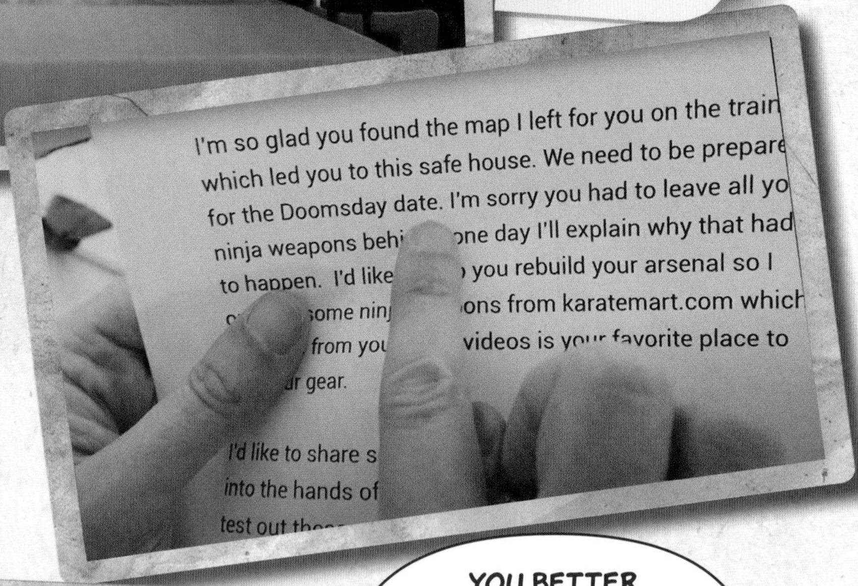

YOU BETTER WATCH OUT, MR. FRUIT! I CAN'T TELL IF HE'S AFRAID OR NOT, SINCE HE DOESN'T HAVE ANY GOOGLY EYES . . .

Hidden inside the fruit, there is a secret message!

The best part of this mystery box is that the Spy Ninjas now have a box full of NINJA WEAPONS to protect themselves while they're on the run from the hackers!

The next morning, while they're watching their spy cam footage of the mystery figure that dropped off the surprise box, they realize that a HACKER KIDNAPPED whoever it was that dropped off the box!

TOP SECRET

If this mystery person was trying to help them, whoever it is must be a friend. Chad and Vy decide now it's THEIR turn to help a friend in trouble, so they set off on a mission into the desert to try to rescue the mystery helper. Once they find him, tied up and left for dead in the desert, they realize it's the LIE DETECTOR EXPERT!

I WAS COMING TO YOUR HOUSE TO WARN YOU ABOUT THE HACKERS, AND THE NEXT THING I KNOW, I WAS THROWN INTO A CAR!

While they're trying to untie the lie detector guy, the Spy Ninjas are confronted by a hacker!

But Chad's not one to give up without a fight. So he and the hacker battle each other using ninja weapons. Chad defeats the hacker in a crazy ninja battle royale!

Now that he's safe with Vy and Chad, the lie detector expert reveals his name is Daniel. He confesses that he's an ex-Project Zorgo hacker who went by the code name **PZ1**.

EX PROJECT ZORGO Member Takes LIE DETECTOR TEST & Face Reveal!

Daniel takes a lie detector test and shows them a video that proves he quit the organization and he is now trying to HELP Chad and Vy defeat the hackers. He warns the Spy Ninjas that something called the **"Doomsday Date"** is getting close, and they have to act fast to stop it. What is the DOOMSDAY DATE?

THE DAY PROJECT ZORGO WILL DESTROY YOUTUBE FOREVER.

Daniel shows the Spy Ninjas news footage that shows that their house was burned down after they fled the hackers. By leaving them all those notes and clues that warned them to GET OUT, Daniel saved Chad and Vy's lives! He really must be a true good guy.

THE BLACK PYRAMID

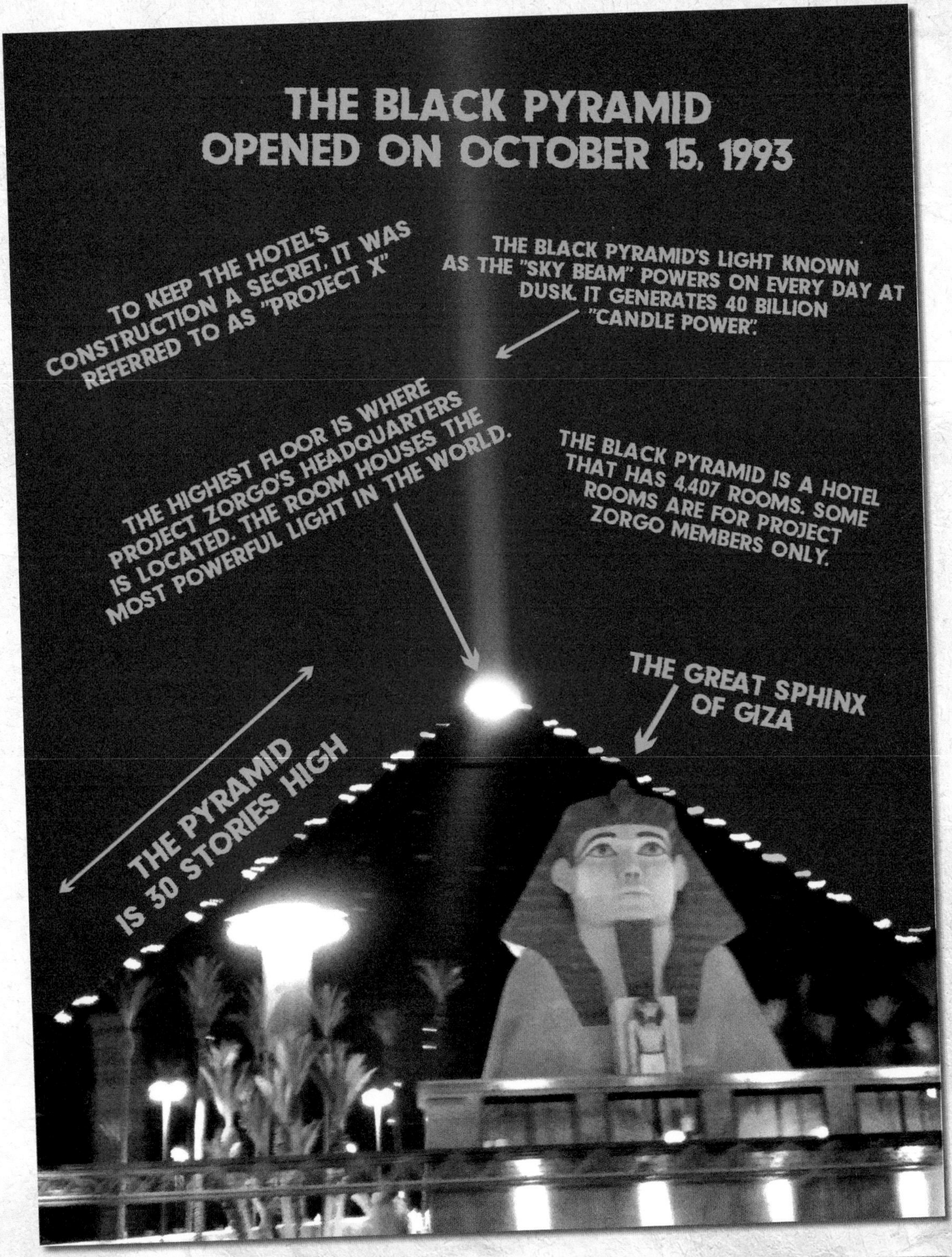

THE BLACK PYRAMID OPENED ON OCTOBER 15, 1993

TO KEEP THE HOTEL'S CONSTRUCTION A SECRET, IT WAS REFERRED TO AS "PROJECT X"

THE BLACK PYRAMID'S LIGHT KNOWN AS THE "SKY BEAM" POWERS ON EVERY DAY AT DUSK. IT GENERATES 40 BILLION "CANDLE POWER".

THE HIGHEST FLOOR IS WHERE PROJECT ZORGO'S HEADQUARTERS IS LOCATED. THE ROOM HOUSES THE MOST POWERFUL LIGHT IN THE WORLD.

THE BLACK PYRAMID IS A HOTEL THAT HAS 4,407 ROOMS. SOME ROOMS ARE FOR PROJECT ZORGO MEMBERS ONLY.

THE GREAT SPHINX OF GIZA

THE PYRAMID IS 30 STORIES HIGH

TOP SECRET

PROJECT ZORGO HEADQUARTERS!!

After intercepting a box from a hacker, Chad and Vy find a map that leads them to THE BLACK PYRAMID in Las Vegas—where they're hoping to break into Project Zorgo HQ!

Chad tries to take the elevator to the top of the pyramid because he believes that is where the Project Zorgo leader runs the hacker operations . . . but while he's trying to sneak up there, he gets trapped and beaten up by hackers!

TRAPPED IN ELEVATOR at PROJECT ZORGO Headquarters

Vy goes undercover, hoping that if she pretends to be a Project Zorgo hacker, she will be able to find and rescue Chad.

DID YOU KNOW?

When Vy goes undercover as a hacker, she tries to act bigger and older so nobody suspects her true identity.

I ATTEND SECRET PROJECT ZORGO MEETING

During her meeting as an undercover hacker, Vy is put through a series of tests to make sure she's legit. She must spell out the word *NUCLEAR* using the secret Project Zorgo language.

Could YOU pass this challenge?

Luckily, Vy gets all the letters correct, except one.

Do YOU know which of these she got wrong?

N = ⬇️ U = 🔨 C = 👂

L = ⌛ E = ➡️ A = 🔒

R = ▲

ANSWER: R is wrong. R ≠ ▲.

After Vy gets a letter wrong, PZ Leader tells her she must take off her mask and reveal her identity. But it turns out this demand is actually her final test.

Test your SPY NINJA knowledge: What does Vy say to pass the test?

FUN FACT:

The Project Zorgo language frequently changes. In this instance, I believe R = ♣.

ANSWER: "A true Project Zorgo member never reveals their identity."

Meanwhile, as Vy gathers clues and intel, Chad is stuck inside the PROJECT ZORGO JAIL!

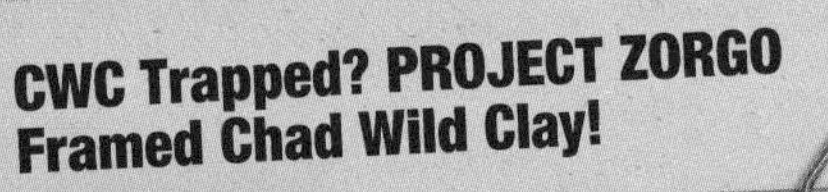

In this horrible cell, Chad discovers a document that makes him realize Project Zorgo is trying to control his mind and brainwash him into becoming a Project Zorgo member!

Luckily, Vy finds Chad and busts him out just in time.

DOOMSDAY

The Doomsday Date has finally arrived. Despite Chad and Vy's best efforts, Project Zorgo has successfully managed to hack into both Chad's and Vy's channels, along with thousands of other YouTubers. But Vy figures out they have one last chance to stop them from a total YouTube takeover:

If they can get a million people to type "Zorgo DIFFUSE" in the comments section of their favorite YouTube channels, they might be able to stop the hackers' evil plot.

The plan works! Thanks to the effort of all their subscribers, the Spy Ninjas are able to overload Project Zorgo's servers and save YouTube from this terrible fate:

SAFE HOUSE TAKEOVER

After the Doomsday Date has been stopped, Chad, Vy, and the newest Spy Ninja team member—**DANIEL**—discover a hidden camera in the Spy Ninjas' **SAFE HOUSE**.

They can't figure out how the camera got there, so they decide to check their security footage. That's when they discover that hackers have found their location and have managed to break into the safe house!

Thankfully, nobody was home when they snuck in, which means there's no proof that Chad, Vy, and Daniel live there. But then, one day, a few weeks later, several mysterious people—a plumber, a delivery driver, and a pizza delivery girl—show up at the safe house and take pictures of the Spy Ninjas. When they open their pizza box, they discover something even weirder: The delivery girl took a triangle-shaped bite out of their order!

What could this possibly mean?

After analyzing the hackers' cameras and decoding what's on the film, Vy reveals to her teammates that Project Zorgo has plans to TAKE OVER their safe house on January 12—the very next day!

After a huge battle to protect the location of the safe house, Chad, Vy, and Daniel finally get home. But as soon as they're locked up inside, they realize they're surrounded by hackers, and the Spy Ninjas don't have any choice except to flee. They're totally outnumbered, and the electronics in the house are going crazy . . . again!

After Daniel takes down one of the hackers during battle, the Spy Ninjas stop to make sure their opponent is okay. Some might wonder: Is the Spy Ninjas' kindness a VIRTUE . . . or a WEAKNESS?

What do YOU think?

DUDE, YOU'RE OKAY, THOUGH?

If YOU were surrounded by a group of hackers, would you:

A) Fight?

B) Run?

C) Scream for backup?

D) Stop to assist if one of your attackers looked like they were hurt and needed help?

JOSEPH BANKS AND THE DELOREAN

Now that the group has nowhere to live, they are forced to stay in their Tesla. But then, one day, the Tesla vanishes, and Daniel gets a strange voice mail from someone who claims to have stolen it.

A mysterious scientist named Joseph Banks reveals HE was the one who stole their Tesla. He's transformed it into a hacker-proof DeLorean! It emits a high-pitched frequency that messes with the electronics in the hackers' masks, which hurts them when they get close to the car. It's a hacker-proof Tesla!

HACKER CAR CHASE! Extreme Makeover of Tesla into a DeLorean

Before Banks takes off, he offers a warning: Do not press this red button. Unfortunately, hackers appear on the scene before Banks has a chance to explain WHY . . . so Chad and Vy are left wondering: What's the deal with the red button??

If YOU were a Spy Ninja, would you:

A) Press the button?

B) Follow Banks's instructions?

SPY NINJA NETWORK

After getting hacked out of their SECOND safe house, Chad and Vy decide to develop something they call the **SPY NINJA NETWORK**, an app that allows their subscribers and fellow SPY NINJAS to help them destroy hacker viruses and send in tips when they see something suspicious or uncover a clue.

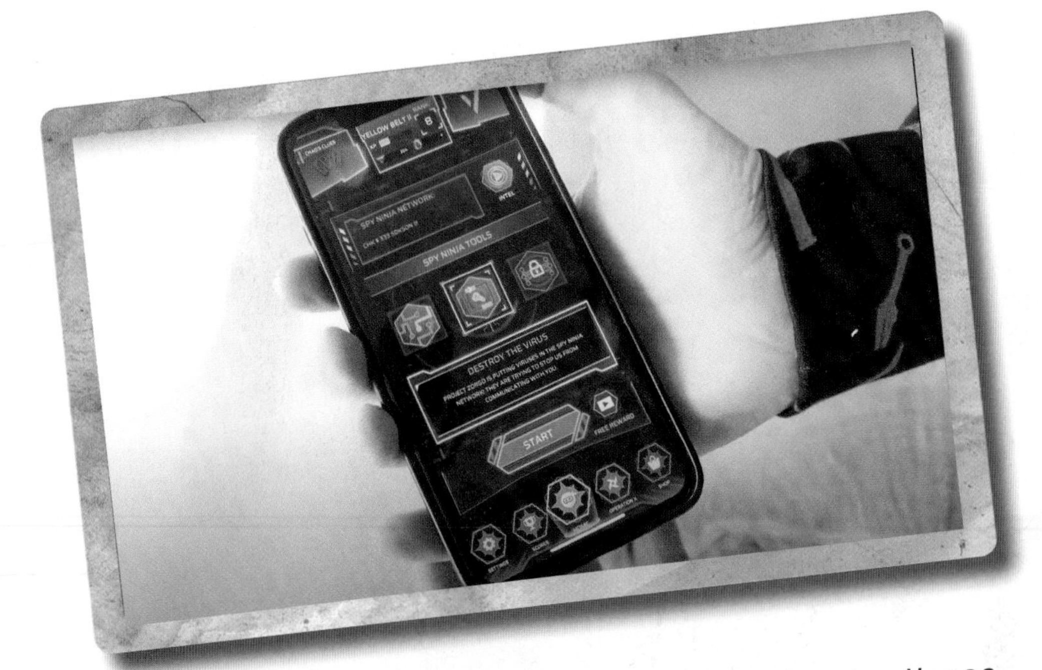

Unfortunately, when the hackers took over the Vegas safe house, they also got access to the two CONTROL KEYS for the SPY NINJA NETWORK. Luckily, Vy is tiny enough to sneak into the safe house access tunnel and steal the keys back from the hackers!

WHO IS PZ4?

After he's been a part of the Spy Ninja team for a while, Daniel starts acting suspicious. He's been getting messages from someone on his Apple Watch, but he won't admit it or tell Chad and Vy who he is communicating with.

DID YOU KNOW?

PZ4 was Daniel's Most Trusted Colleague when he was a member of Project Zorgo.

People watching Daniel's YouTube channel soon learn that he's been talking with one of the hackers—his ex-Project Zorgo coworker **PZ4**—who says she wants to help him!

Daniel Meets with Hacker PZ4

The Spy Ninjas are suspicious of PZ4's motives, but she proves her loyalty to Daniel by THROWING HER HACKER MASK at an incoming KUNAI that is thrown at him by one of the other Project Zorgo members. After that act of bravery, Chad, Vy, and Daniel embark on a quest to figure out who the mysterious PZ4 is and what she's up to.

Meanwhile, every member of Project Zorgo is also hunting for PZ4 since she broke Project Zorgo rules. They must terminate her from the organization because she took her mask off and helped one of the Spy Ninjas.

PROJECT ZORGO'S #1 RULE:
Never take off your mask!

TO Daniel / PZ1,

PLese don't share this with anybody! especially the SPY NINJAS. Chad & Vy! My days at Project Zorgo are probably over & I'm in BIG trouble. When I saved you by blocking the kunai with my mask, I broke the #1 rule of Project Zorgo, never take off your mask. Now I know how you feel when you were on the run from PZ. I know how to fix this. I know a place we can stay & be safe. It'll be our safe house in the middle of Las Vegas. It's got an awesome pool, a tennis court, and a ~~secret~~ hatch. If you don't reply to this in a few days, I'll try to make contact with you through your apple watch... but that'll be pretty risky. DON'T SHOW THIS TO ANYBODY!!!

PZ4

The other hackers have turned on her, so now PZ4 is on the run. The Spy Ninjas know they need to figure out who this PZ4 person is so that they can help her. She is Daniel's closest colleague after all, and even more important, she saved his life! After the Spy Ninjas battle with a Project Zorgo member called PZ9, he reveals the location of where the hackers are keeping and torturing PZ4.

Vy sneaks in and rescues PZ4, and the two of them make a getaway in the DeLorean! Go, Vy!

NEW SAFE HOUSE

As a way of saying thank you, PZ4 gives Chad, Vy, and Daniel a place to stay—and it's absolutely epic. This new SAFE HOUSE has a POOL, a HOT TUB, and a TENNIS COURT!

But . . . there is one secret room PZ4 says the Spy Ninjas must never enter.

If YOU were a member of the Spy Ninjas, would YOU enter the room?

YES or NO

TOP SECRET

Project Zorgo is really upset with PZ4 for betraying them, so she's still on the run.

Project Zorgo devises a plan to frame PZ4 for a crime she didn't do so she'll get ARRESTED BY THE POLICE!

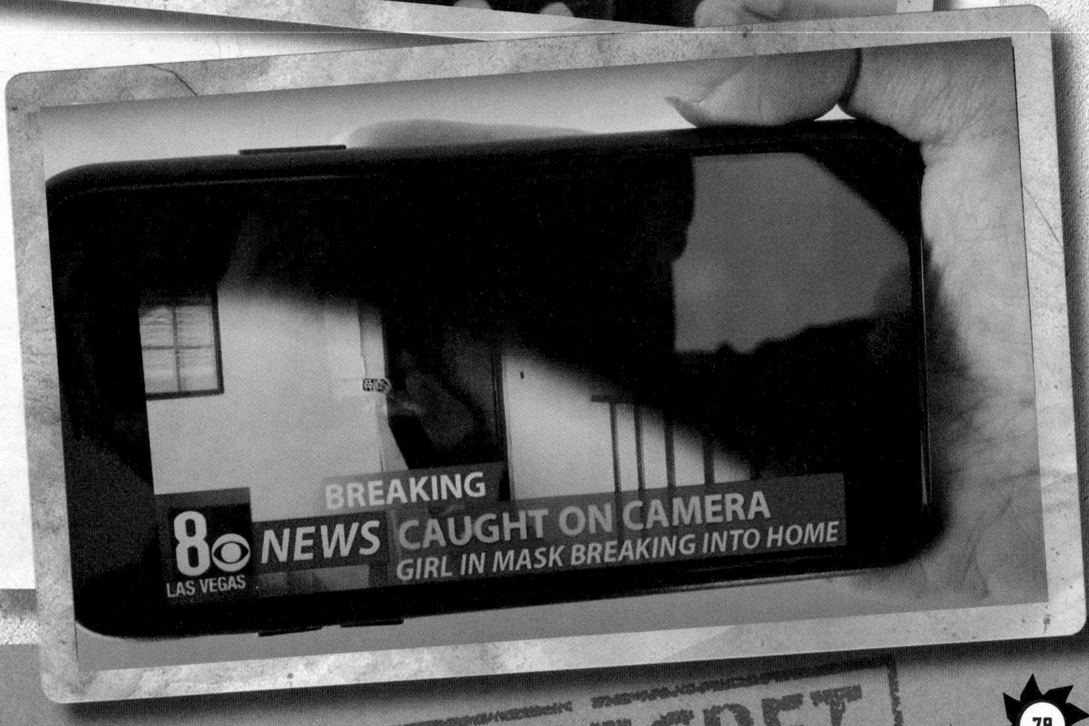

HACKER GIRL IS WANTED BY THE POLICE

While she's trying to prove PZ4's innocence using stolen surveillance video, Vy is also ARRESTED—since the video shows that she was at the crime scene with PZ4, too!

VY QWAINT ARRESTED and FRAMED by PROJECT ZORGO While Trying to Rescue HACKER GIRL PZ4!

Daniel and Chad help break the girls out of jail, and during the process of rescuing them, they learn that PZ4's real name is REGINA!

THE SIGNAL BOOSTER

The Spy Ninjas steal a device called the SIGNAL BOOSTER from Project Zorgo. They find out that it's a new hacker tool that will allow them to hack into ANY YouTuber's channel as long as they're within a one-mile radius of the signal booster. The Spy Ninjas have to make sure Project Zorgo never gets to use their signal booster! Or who knows what they will be capable of?!

Unfortunately, Project Zorgo manages to steal the Signal Booster back. While the Spy Ninjas are hunting for the signal booster, they find some wooden sticks that all have a weird Project Zorgo secret language on them. They realize that if they could decode the message, they might be able to figure out what type of evil plot Project Zorgo is planning to use the Signal Booster for. Luckily, they have their Spy Ninja DECODER and they're able to use it to decode the messages!

HACKER GIRL UNMASKED in NINJA BATTLE ROYALE

Meanwhile, Regina's mask starts making a strange beeping sound. The beeping gets faster and faster, until the mask EXPLODES into a dozen little pieces and crumbles away to reveal REGINA's REAL FACE for the first time ever!

TEST YOUR SPY NINJA KNOWLEDGE!

After Regina's mask explodes, they wrap her face in bandages so it can heal, and they set up a series of challenges to test her Spy Ninja readiness. If she succeeds in completing their challenges, Regina will officially reveal her face and become the newest SPY NINJA!

SPY TEST:

If you were faced with these challenges, how would YOU fare?

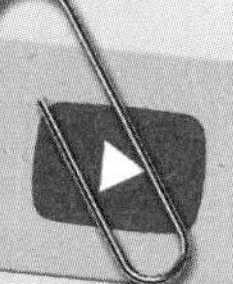

FACE REVEAL of HACKER GIRL REGINA PZ4 – Unmasking Spy Ninja Challenge

CHALLENGE #1: Kick a board in half.

If you had to complete this challenge, would you try to break the board with a FRONT KICK (like Vy) . . .

or a ROUNDHOUSE KICK (like Regina)?

CHALLENGE #2: Trivia

Who was the Spy Ninjas' first cameraperson?

A) Daniel
B) Justin
C) Vy
D) Chad

ANSWER: Justin

CHALLENGE #3: Lie-Detecting Challenge

Do you think YOU would be able to tell which Spy Ninja was lying about which box Daniel's Apple Watch is hidden inside? Would you trust your skills enough to SMASH one of the boxes, based on your lie detecting skills?

CHALLENGE #4: Trivia

ANSWER: The hairs on the back of her neck stand up!

CHALLENGE #5:

Trivia

WHAT WAS THE FIRST NINJA
GADGET DANIEL HELD?

ANSWER: Futuristic ninja machete

CHALLENGE #6:

Ninja Move Challenge

Regina must dodge all Vy's shots, to prove she has ninja agility.

CHALLENGE FAIL

SECRET

CHALLENGE #7:
Trivia

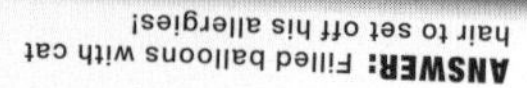

ANSWER: Filled balloons with cat hair to set off his allergies!

CHALLENGE #8:
Trivia

What were Regina's answers?

ANSWER: BRAVERY, HONESTY, LOYALTY

Regina passes the tests, so her face wrap can come off. She's officially a SPY NINJA now!

DID YOU KNOW?

Regina unmasked herself and officially became a Spy Ninja on May 26, 2019.

PZ4 IS NO MORE!

REGINA'S BEST DISGUISES

IS JUSTIN . . . PZ9?!

In order to find out the next big hacker event Project Zorgo is planning, Daniel pretends to rejoin Project Zorgo. Welcome back, PZ1!

While he's undercover, Daniel finds out that Project Zorgo needs the hacker called PZ9 to lead their next hacking mission. But PZ9 has been missing for months!

The Spy Ninjas have a theory that PZ9 could possibly be Chad's old childhood friend Justin—after all, PZ9 is an amazing fighter (just like Chad and Justin), he has a beard like Justin's, and he has excellent bo staff skills like Chad's childhood pal! The Spy Ninjas know they need to find PZ9 before Project Zorgo does, or they're in a whole lot of trouble.

While hunting for PZ9, Daniel stumbles upon the missing hacker in a cursed old spirit tunnel. He seems more evil than ever and has a scary new look.

The Spy Ninjas battle him and try to unmask him, but PZ9 gets away—again.

They decide the only way to figure out if Justin really is PZ9 is to follow him and see if they can uncover any clues. In the process, the Spy Ninjas finally figure out how to decode the secret language on the wooden sticks they found weeks ago.

Remember that clue?
Have you been paying attention to
ALL the clues along the way?

The sticks spell out:

CREATOR GATHERING: ANAHEIM, CALIFORNIA, WEDNESDAY, JULY 10!

That's when the Spy Ninjas realize that the huge event Project Zorgo is planning to hack: They're going after hundreds of YouTubers that will be attending VIDCON, with PZ9 leading the mission.

TOP SECRET

VIDCON HACK

After months of working as a fake undercover Project Zorgo member, Daniel is finally caught by PZ9 and outed as a double agent.

DANIEL ARRESTED by HACKERS & REVEALED AS SPY NINJA

Now that the Spy Ninjas' plans are ruined and Daniel can no longer get insider info as a Project Zorgo spy, PZ9 and the Zorgo members are successful in their quest to HACK VIDCON!

The Spy Ninja channels are hacked, along with dozens of other YouTubers. Project Zorgo has taken over!

CONFIDENTIAL

June 3 2019.
ATTENTION ALL PROJECT ZORGO MEMBERS

DO NOT SHARE this document with anybody outside the Project Zorgo organization. It is crucial content creators of YouTube are unaware of the events that will take place on July 10th, 2019 in Anahiem California.

Thousands of YouTubers from around the globe will be attending Vidcon 2019. So many YouTubers in one spot is unprecedented. We must take this opportunity to hack every creator who attends the event.

With a Black Tesla Model 3 and the Signal Booster we will be able to hack and delete every attendee's YouTube channel.

CONFIDENTIAL

For us to pull this off, we will need PZ9, our best fighter to lead the mission. PZ9 has been missing for months. If any Project Zorgo member has information of PZ9's whereabouts, please let PZ2 or PZ 18 know.

MY YOUTUBE IS HACKED!

Luckily, thanks to some clever problem-solving and clue hunting, the Spy Ninjas eventually regain control of their channels by stealing Project Zorgo's emergency shutdown buttons.

I SAVED VIDCON & STOPPED PROJECT ZORGO HACKER PZ9 FROM HACKING 10,000 YOUTUBERS

During the mission, PZ9 got selfish and ABANDONED his fellow Project Zorgo members. He stole the YOUTUBE SOURCE CODE because he wanted to claim all the glory for shutting down YouTube forever, all by himself!

The Spy Ninjas aren't going to let this guy get away with it, though. So Chad, Vy, Regina, and Daniel track him down. They watch as PZ9 walks into a Burger King . . . and stare in horror when, moments later, their friend JUSTIN walks out! The Spy Ninjas are convinced the hacker PZ9 must be their friend Justin. Does that make Justin . . . one of the BAD GUYS?!

Project Zorgo members and PZ9 are not getting along now that PZ9 has betrayed them. But PZ9 still has the YouTube source code. Which means the Spy Ninjas need to find PZ9 before Project Zorgo does so they can get it back! But even after Chad masks up and pretends to be PZ9 to try to throw Project Zorgo off the trail, other PZ members manage to find PZ9 and battle him . . . and in the process, the disk with the source code is destroyed!

At the end of the battle, Project Zorgo members unmask PZ9 and take his uniform.

For missions like tracking down PZ9, Vy always brings her SPY ESSENTIALS KIT. What kinds of things are in a Spy Ninja's kit?

- Decoder Wheel
- Ninja Noise Enhancer
- Secret Message Pen

TEST YOUR SPY NINJA DETECTIVE SKILLS!

Can you tell which one is the REAL PZ9, and which one is Chad Wild Clay in a PZ9 disguise?

Now that Project Zorgo has UNMASKED PZ9, the Spy Ninjas know they are searching for someone in plain clothes—not someone in a Zorgo mask. When they spot their friend JUSTIN, wearing plain clothes and beating up Project Zorgo members, it makes them even MORE certain that their pal Justin must be PZ9.

But then, after Chad gets captured by hackers and is handcuffed to a fence . . .

. . . it's his old pal Justin who comes to his rescue!

While the other Spy Ninjas watch through Daniel's drone, Justin takes on a hacker and FREES CHAD from his cuffs.

CWC vs. BEST FRIEND BATTLE ROYALE Challenge to Learn if Hacker PZ9 is Justin

The Spy Ninjas finally realize that Justin can't possibly be PZ9, since he SAVED CHAD from Project Zorgo. That means Justin must be one of the good guys!

But if JUSTIN isn't PZ9 . . . who IS? Before they can figure that out, Daniel's drone catches the end of a Project Zorgo meeting, where the REAL PZ9 offers other PZ members **$10,000** for each Spy Ninja they capture and take prisoner!

TOP SECRET!

With this kind of threat looming over them, the Spy Ninjas know it's time to figure out, once and for all, who this mysterious PZ9 is. After some spy work and clue-solving, the Spy Ninjas reveal PZ9's true name is:

GOODBYE, VY?!

After PZ9 separates from Project Zorgo, this PZ member reveals that Vy has a huge SECRET she's been hiding from the other Spy Ninjas. The Spy Ninjas have to compete in a series of challenges in order to convince PZ9 to tell Vy's secret.

With each successful challenge, they get another piece of the puzzle.

Regina and Vy get into a huge fight over Vy's secrecy, and Vy starts wondering if maybe it's time to tell someone what she's been hiding. After all, honesty is one of the most important parts of being a Spy Ninja. But she's keeping this secret from them for their own good!

The Spy Ninjas decide they need to spy on Vy, hoping they might be able to find out what sort of secret she's been hiding from them.

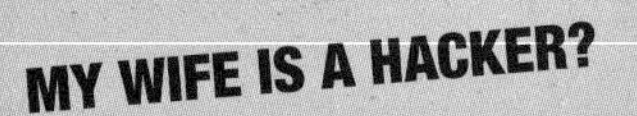

Vy Qwaint has betrayed the spy ninjas. She has been working with Project Zorgo for the past three months behind your backs. 7.20 14:00

They discover that Vy has secretly been working as a Project Zorgo hacker for six months . . . and no one knew!

VY QWAINT IS WORKING WITH PROJECT ZORGO?!

VY QWAINT LEAVES SPY NINJAS SAFE HOUSE!
YOU HAVE TO TRUST ME. YOU'LL SEE ME AGAIN, I PROMISE.
KICKED OUT OF SPY NINJAS!

THE RED SAFE

Eventually, Vy reveals to the rest of the team that she went UNDERCOVER AS A PROJECT ZORGO MEMBER to TRICK the hackers into giving her a top secret item: the Red Safe! She's been told that what's inside the safe will defeat Project Zorgo forever.

That's UNDERCOVER VY!

The Spy Ninjas can't get the safe open, no matter how many times they try—using brute force, Ninja tools, smarts, and general common sense.

Project Zorgo wants their safe back SO BAD that they capture PZ9 and try to use him for leverage to get what they want. They offer the Spy Ninjas a deal: Turn in the Red Safe, or they'll use a special tool to force PZ9 to tell them the location of the Spy Ninjas' safe house.

The Spy Ninjas decide to keep the safe—Vy worked too hard to get it to give it back now, and they all hope they'll eventually figure out how to crack it open to get whatever's inside.

If you were a Spy Ninja, what would YOU do?

A) Return the safe, in order to protect the Spy Ninja safe house at all costs.

B) Risk the safety of the safe house, in order to keep the safe Vy worked so hard—as a secret double agent—to get from Project Zorgo!

TOP SECRET

ERASED MEMORIES

Project Zorgo still has PZ9 in their control. While he's their prisoner, they cruelly ERASE PZ9's MEMORY of the past year for revenge because he betrayed the other PZ members at VidCon. With his recent memory gone, PZ9 rejoins Project Zorgo again—because he's forgotten why he left the hacker group in the first place.

When the Spy Ninjas realize what's been done to PZ9, they discover that DANIEL'S MEMORY WAS ERASED when he joined Project Zorgo! He can't remember his mom, his dog, or even that he used to play music on his YouTube channel!

When Regina finally allows the Spy Ninjas to go inside her SECRET ROOM (the one they've been told never to enter, for any reason), the Spy Ninjas discover something important: Regina's memory was ALSO erased when she joined Project Zorgo! All the photos of friends and family in her room aren't real—they've all been photoshopped to give Regina FAKE MEMORIES!

And while they're trying to dig into Regina's REAL history, the Spy Ninjas discover the craziest surprise of all . . .
PZ9 is REGINA'S BROTHER!

Kid Regina!

Kid PZ9!

PZ9 IS MY BROTHER?
TOP SECRET

IS PZ9 . . . A FRIEND?

As soon as they learn that PZ9 is Regina's brother,
PZ9 starts to act friendly toward the Spy Ninjas.
What is going on?! The Spy Ninjas actually start to
consider inviting PZ9 to join their group—if he's
Regina's family, maybe he's meant to be one of the
good guys.

But then, weeks after they start to welcome him into
the group, PZ9 reveals his true colors . . . the Spy
Ninjas learn he's been TRICKING THEM to try to steal
Chad's 10,000,000 Subscriber YouTube play button!

PZ9 BETRAYS The SPY NINJAS

Eventually, PZ9 starts to feel guilty for betraying his new friends. He ends up bonding with Daniel over having their memories erased when they joined Project Zorgo, and he grows closer to his sister, Regina. Then, finally, he apologizes to the Spy Ninjas.

PZ9 is SORRY for LEAVING SPY NINJAS

It takes a while, but the Spy Ninjas finally decide that PZ9 can be their friend . . . though only if he does a face reveal and proves he deserves a place on the team. So the Spy Ninjas set up a fun challenge that forces PZ9 to prove he has what it takes to join their team. Would YOU pass the test? Let's see how much you remember from PZ9's Face Reveal Challenge . . .

TOP SECRET

WHAT WAS VY TRYING TO OBTAIN AS AN UNDERCOVER HACKER?

ANSWER: The Red Safe.

PZ9 HAS TO USE FRUIT NINJA SKILLS TO CHOP WHAT KIND OF FRUIT INTO A BUNCH OF PIECES?

ANSWER: Watermelon

PZ9 SHOWS OFF HIS NINJA SKILLS BY PERFORMING A SERIES OF MOVES AND KICKS TO SHOW HE'S GOT THE PHYSICAL SKILLS ALL SPY NINJAS NEED. PUT TOGETHER YOUR OWN NINJA ROUTINE TO DEMONSTRATE YOUR OLYMPIC SPY NINJA SKILLS!

PZ9 HAS TO CHOP THREE SODA BOTTLES IN HALF TO PROVE HE HAS SPY NINJA CHOPPING SKILLS. WHAT COLOR ARE THE THREE SODAS?

ANSWER: Red, green, and orange

ANSWER: (B) Squirt Blaster

PZ9 PASSES THE TEST, AND FINALLY HIS MASK COMES OFF.

AFTER HIS MASK IS GONE AND HE PASSES A LIE DETECTOR TEST TO ENSURE HE'S BEING FULLY HONEST, PZ9 BECOMES AN OFFICIAL SPY NINJA, AND THEY START TO CALL HIM BY HIS REAL NAME: **MELVIN!**

COME BACK CHAD

Chad you're dull! You've become such
a snooze!
If we have to battle hackers...
We'll probably lose!

Yeah he's so bland, and just so vanilla, like
PZZ's favorite cheese-less quesadilla!

I know what to do, yeah I figured
it out. Chad join my class.
Ninja Moves for Clout!!!!!....

They really messed with Chad,
YEAH he's not the same.
He got ZAAPPED
now he's BORING
and LAME!!

When I get out of bed I need to take a rest
I look in the mirror and have a staring contest
I like my dentist but he wasn't polite
When I said I've been flossing...
...in Fortnite

Chad! Your mind!
Turned into mashed potatos
Now it's time!

Kick bump! Do some tornado kicks
and flips!
Just like the guy you used to be
You see?
Looks like youre scaring Vy!

Come back Chad! The one we always had!
Come back Chad! Without you were so sad
Chad's a Snore!
You use to be so hyper
314 is cooler even wearing diapers

TOP SECRET

REACHING THE TOP OF THE PYRAMID

For years the Spy Ninjas have been trying to reach the top of the Black Pyramid where Project Zorgo's headquarters is located. They trained and trained and finally they were ready. They went through the weather room that gets super hot and super cold, crawled through the vent, and found the elevator that took them to the top. They finally made it and escaped just before the PZ Leader captured them!

PROJECT ZORGO'S THREAT IS REAL!

REGINA'S CHANNEL GOT DELETED!

Project Zorgo is becoming stronger and a serious threat. They delete Regina's entire YouTube channel with over 1 million subscribers and all the videos she had on it.

Melvin goes missing, and we haven't seen him for 2 weeks! Suddenly, Project Zorgo uploads a video saying they have finally defeated Melvin and he is no longer living.

Project Zorgo also announces that on December 31, New Year's Eve, once the clock strikes midnight, YouTube will be deleted forever. As the world is lighting off fireworks to celebrate a new year, Project Zorgo will be celebrating their victory! The Spy Ninjas are horrified. First they delete Regina's channel, then kill Melvin, and now delete YouTube? They take this threat seriously and realize ENOUGH IS ENOUGH. It's time to end Project Zorgo forever.

MR. E

The Spy Ninjas receive a mysterious phone call from someone named MR. E. Even though the Spy Ninjas have no idea who this MR. E is, they decide to follow the clues he gives them, which lead them on some crazy adventures around the world to find their real families. Daniel hops on a plane to New York City, hoping to rescue his dog, Douglas, from hackers.

But when Daniel gets back to Las Vegas with Douglas's crate, he discovers that, sometime during his mission, someone swapped his real dog for a STUFFED dog! Who has DOUGLAS?!

Just so you all know! The PZ announcement that Melvin is dead was just a trick!

Melvin sets off for the Philippines to try to track down his grandparents. During his journey, he discovers his grandparents are dead! But while he's in the Philippines, he bumps into even more Project Zorgo hackers—are these guys everywhere?!

Meanwhile, Regina heads to California to try to find her parents. She follows a series of clues from Mr. E, and eventually gets to her mom's house—but before she can talk with her, Regina is captured by even more hackers!

Eventually, the other Spy Ninjas head to California and rescue her. But after bumping into PZ members in so many places around the world, they're all a little worried about how big the Project Zorgo organization has gotten . . . hackers are EVERYWHERE!

TOP SECRET

THE SECRET HATCH

Months after Regina lets her fellow Spy Ninjas into her secret room, Melvin is hanging out in there one day and bumps his head on something metal that's been hidden under a tablecloth! The other Spy Ninjas come in to check it out and discover it's some sort of SECRET HATCH! Where does this hatch lead, and what's behind the door?!

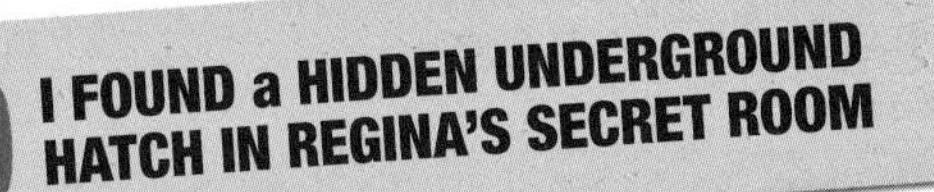

Regina won't let anyone open the door to see what's behind it. But when everyone is asleep, Melvin sneaks in her room—he's determined to find out what Regina's been hiding all this time!

After months of trying to figure out the mystery of the hatch, the Spy Ninjas finally get inside and find a huge room on the other side of the door, which goes down 300 feet!

BENEATH OUR SAFEHOUSE

Yikes! Even stranger, they discover that someone named **PERLITA** has been living under their safe house for years.

Creepy? Definitely.

But it's certainly not the strangest thing that's ever happened—or will ever happen—to the Spy Ninja team!

TOP SECRET

After nearly two years of protecting their current safe house from hackers and successfully holding off Project Zorgo, I'll never forget the day that marked the beginning of the end . . . the day Chad, Vy, and the team faced the ultimate showdown against dozens of Project Zorgo hackers!

One day, the team spotted a group of PZ members sneaking up on the safe house. Vy could see that there were a lot of them. And she knew right away that the time had come for a *massive battle* to protect their safe house and BEAT Project Zorgo, once and for all!

HACKERS STOLE OUR HOUSE!
THIS IS OUR SAFE HOUSE! SO, PULL YOU LIP OVER YOUR FACE, AND SWALLOW!
TOP SECRET

When Daniel uses his Spy Ninja Noise Enhancer, he realizes that there are even *more* hackers on their way—and if they don't finish this off, right now . . . it's gonna be game over for the Spy Ninjas!

The Spy Ninjas load up a slingshot with all kinds of missiles, trying to take down the hackers when they're least expecting it.

TOP SECRET

If YOU were a Spy Ninja trying to defeat Project Zorgo hackers, which of these things would YOU choose to load into the slingshot first?

1) Plastic balls
2) Bag of onions
3) Soccer ball
4) Rubber chicken
5) Pumpkin

But just when the Spy Ninjas think they have things under control, Project Zorgo brings in reinforcements . . . and the Spy Ninjas are so outnumbered they can't fight back. It's time to flee . . .

TOP SECRET

THIS IS PROJECT ZORGO'S
SAFE HOUSE NOW!

safehouse now

But the Spy Ninjas have NO plans to just give up. It's time to:

TAKE OUR SAFEHOUSE BACK!

FIRST STEP: Get their DeLorean back.

WE GOT THE DELOREAN!

SECOND STEP: Try to get back all their Spy Ninja gadgets. (No one can fight hackers without Spy Ninja gear!)

THIRD STEP: Take back the safe house.

FOURTH STEP: STOP PROJECT ZORGO from completing their ultimate mission: **TAKING OVER YOUTUBE**!

Luckily, the Spy Ninjas bump into Perlita, who thinks she can help them put their plan into action!

She leads the team to a secret tunnel—and tells them it's the one she uses to get in and out of her hidden room under the safe house!

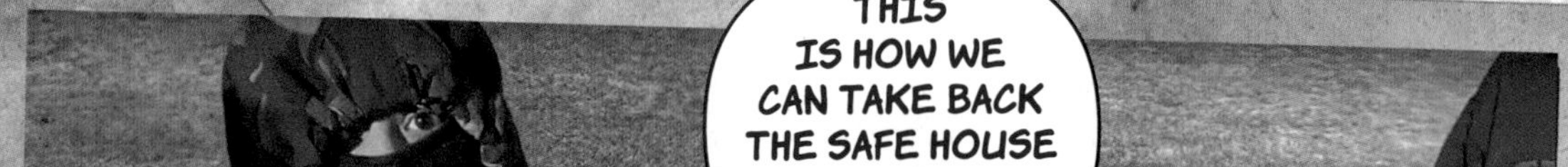

But when they get inside Regina's room in the safe house, the Spy Ninjas realize there are way too many hackers in the house for them to fight and survive. So Chad devises a new plan:

They realize they can set off the anti-hacker signal in the car and scare Project Zorgo out of the house! Everyone is willing to try it. They know they have to do something and are ready to fight for their house and the future of YouTube!

TOP SECRET

WE LOST . . . Project Zorgo Wins. Battle Royale vs. Hackers for Safe House after Hiding Underground

But even with their incredible Ninja fighting skills, this plan doesn't work. There are just too many hackers for the four of them to take on. After an epic and hard-fought fight, Project Zorgo captures the team, and it's starting to look like this is the end of Spy Ninjas . . .

But then!

Melvin—who's been missing for months (and some people even thought he was dead!)—shows up just in time and helps the team take down dozens of hackers in the most epic Spy Ninja battle royale EVER! It's finally time to take back the safe house and stop Project Zorgo FOR GOOD!

With the whole team back together, the Spy Ninjas are unstoppable! Doomsday has officially arrived for Project Zorgo . . . YouTube is no longer threatened, and the Spy Ninjas are the ULTIMATE CHAMPIONS in their years-long battle against the evil hacking group Project Zorgo!

TOP SECRET

THE END

The day has come when Project Zorgo will delete YouTube forever. There's only a few hours left until the clock strikes midnight and YouTube is gone. The Spy Ninjas barge into the Black Pyramid where they will do their final battle. It's now or never. After hundreds of battle royales with the most incredible hacker fighters they've seen, they make it to the final boss—The PZ Leader. He is even taller than before, because he's wearing jumping stilts. The Spy Ninjas try to fight back and after a long battle, they electrocute the leader as they all join together to do a KICKBUMP!

DID YOU KNOW?

The PZ Leader made some interesting sounds during the final fight. Some people say he sounded electronic. Is he a robot? Some say they heard the PZ Leader's voice glitching out as he fell to the ground dying. Rumor has it, if you reverse his glitchy voice there is a secret message.

The leader falls to the ground. An FBI agent named Agent Peters comes onto the scene and pronounces the PZ Leader dead. He covers up the body. The Spy Ninjas leave the Black Pyramid. Finally, after almost three years. Project Zorgo is defeated and YouTube is saved!

So . . . what's next for the **SPY NINJAS?**
No one really knows for sure.

But what I DO know is, it's time for **YOU** to decide: After reviewing this essential Spy Ninja history and studying the details of some of their most action-packed adventures in this book (plus all the missions you've followed on their YouTube channels!), are you WITH the Spy Ninjas . . . or are you AGAINST them?

It's your choice. Just make sure it's the correct one.

I know I have. (And no, I'm still not going to tell you who I am—that kind of ruins the fun, doesn't it? But trust me: You'll find out soon enough when the time is right. A true Spy Ninja never lies.)

Now the world is waiting to find out: What's YOUR next move?